KIDS CAN'T STOP ~~~
THE CHOOSE YOUR
OWN ADVENTURE® STORIES!

"Choose Your Own Adventure is the best thing that has come along since books themselves."
—Alysha Beyer, age 11

"I didn't read much before, but now I read my Choose Your Own Adventure books almost every night."
—Chris Brogan, age 13

"I love the control I have over what happens next."
—Kosta Efstathiou, age 17

"Choose Your Own Adventure books are so much fun to read and collect—I want them all!"
—Brendan Davin, age 11

And teachers like this series, too:
"We have read and reread, worn thin, loved, loaned, bought for others, and donated to school libraries our Choose Your Own Adventure books."

CHOOSE YOUR OWN ADVENTURE®—
AND MAKE READING MORE FUN!

Bantam Books in the Choose Your Own Adventure® series
Ask your bookseller for the books you have missed

ALIEN, GO HOME!

BY SEDDON JOHNSON

ILLUSTRATED BY LESLIE MORRILL

An R.A. Montgomery Book

BANTAM BOOKS
NEW YORK • TORONTO • LONDON • SYDNEY • AUCKLAND

RL 4, age 10 and up

ALIEN, GO HOME!
A Bantam Book / May 1990

*CHOOSE YOUR OWN ADVENTURE® is a registered trademark of
Bantam Books, a division of Bantam Doubleday Dell Publishing Group,
Inc. Registered in U.S. Patent and Trademark Office and elsewhere.*

Original conception of Edward Packard

*Cover art by Romas Kukalis
Interior illustrations by Leslie Morrill*

ISBN 0-553-28482-7

Published simultaneously in the United States and Canada

---

*Bantam Books are published by Bantam Books, a division of Bantam Double-
day Dell Publishing Group, Inc. Its trademark, consisting of the words
"Bantam Books" and the portrayal of a rooster, is Registered in U.S. Patent
and Trademark Office and in other countries. Marca Registrada. Bantam
Books, 666 Fifth Avenue, New York, New York 10103.*

PRINTED IN THE UNITED STATES OF AMERICA

OPM   0 9 8 7 6 5 4 3 2

With all my love, to Doug

WARNING!!!

Do not read this book straight through from beginning to end. These pages contain many different adventures that you may have while you are panning for gold in Canada's Yukon Territory. From time to time as you read along, you will be asked to make a choice. Your choice may lead to success or disaster!

The adventures you have are the results of your choices. You are responsible because you choose! After you make a choice, follow the instructions to see what happens next.

Think carefully before you make a decision. A Soviet space shuttle has mysteriously fallen out of orbit. Somewhere in your search for gold you may come in contact with this spacecraft. And if you do, your new friend could be your new enemy!

Good luck!

You've hitchhiked over six thousand miles and bummed passage on a fishing trawler for another thousand when you finally get up to the "bush" of Canada's Yukon Territory. Sourdough, an old geologist and prospector who was shipmate with you on your uncle Ben's ocean research vessel, the *Pole Star,* has invited you to spend your summer vacation with him—*panning for gold*! His home is an old log cabin, hundreds of miles from the closest town.

While you were on the *Pole Star* last summer, on an expedition to the South Pole, Sourdough spent hours telling you about his mining adventures in the Yukon. You had visions of striking it rich. But so far all you've gotten for your time wading in icy streams and slewing mud around in your gold-mining pan has been a few flecks of gold—"colors" as he calls it. Sourdough kids you about this in a good-natured way, chuckling over how "a gold digger the likes of you can't even earn enough to pay for a stack of pancakes!" Then he slaps his hand on his knee and roars with laughter.

Turn to page 2.

2

During the day, while you're out panning, Sourdough spends his time rambling around in search of the lost Glory Hole gold mine. In the evenings, while he talks on the ham radio to his friends from all over the territory, you realize it takes a special breed of person to live in the Yukon. Like Sourdough always says, "Make one mistake up here and it'll be your last."

You arrive back at the cabin late one afternoon. Sourdough tells you he's been listening to the shortwave radio all day while you've been out.

"Listen to this!" he says. "The Soviet Space Administration has announced that radio contact with their newly developed space shuttle was mysteriously cut off eight hours ago. They reckon the shuttle has fallen out of orbit and is headed way off course. They're unable to figure out whether it will continue on aimlessly into outer space or crashland someplace on Earth!"

You are frying up a couple of moose steaks for dinner when you hear an excited voice on the radio say that the Soviets are now predicting the shuttle will come down somewhere in the Yukon.

Go on to the next page.

You don't waste a minute. "Lend me your binoculars, Sourdough. I'm gonna climb the ridge across from the cabin and set up my own shuttle-tracking station." You jam into your backpack your sleeping bag, a flashlight, a greasy moose sandwich, and a pocket tape player. "If I see anything, I'll signal you in Morse code with the flashlight."

Sourdough shakes his head, amused. "That's plumb like looking for a needle in a haystack," he chortles, "but go on ahead."

Before he can even finish his sentence, you're long gone, headed for the ridge.

You scramble up to the ridge, wolf down your sandwich, and then curl up in the sleeping bag to keep warm. In the Yukon at this time of year, the days are very long. The sun barely dips below the horizon, and the stars are poking out. It all looks so beautiful.

Go on to the next page.

4

Suddenly you see something. A brilliant pin-point of light overhead flares against the gray evening sky, getting larger and brighter. You look through the binoculars—it's the shuttle! You wonder how the cosmonauts can hope to make a safe landing anywhere in this region. Then you realize they must be headed for Cariboo Lake, which is just over the next ridge. You watch as the shuttle descends steadily and finally disappears below the ridge. You prepare yourself for the flash of a huge explosion, but there isn't one.

Quickly you start racing toward the landing site when you remember Sourdough. You should let him know what's happened so he can call the authorities on his radio. You flash a message with your flashlight in the direction of the cabin, but you get no response.

"Come on, Sourdough, wake up!" you yell several times from the ridge. He's probably asleep, you realize. You should run back and get him—you might need his help. On the other hand, the cosmonauts might be hurt. Perhaps you should run to the shuttle as quickly as possible and see if you can lend a hand.

*If you decide to return to the cabin,
turn to page 42.*

*If you decide to run to the shuttle,
turn to page 15.*

As a last-minute thought, you snatch up your camera as you're heading out the door. Who knows—you just might be able to scoop the press with some photos taken at the crash site!

"Slow down," you hear Sourdough wheeze, as he struggles to keep up with you. Together you head up the ridge.

Just as you're about to crest the second ridge, two Canadian jets make low passes into the valley.

"Come on, Sourdough! We've got to get there fast and see if we can be of help."

In a few minutes Cariboo Lake lies before you. "There it is!" you shout. The shuttle has used the entire length of the lakeshore to make its landing, finally crashing into a stand of pine trees. Aluminum and glass are strewn all over the area.

"Surprised the thing didn't blow," Sourdough pants as he regains his breath. "We have to hurry, but we'd better be real careful. With all the spilled fuel and electric sparks zapping around, the thing might explode any second!"

Go on the the next page.

Through the binoculars, you carefully inspect the wreckage. There is a strange glow toward the rear of the shattered fuselage. Frantically you climb down through the shrubs and trees. When you stop for another look, you see the glow is getting brighter. The shuttle must be on fire!

Sourdough looks worried. "If that thing blows, we won't live to tell the story. We should wait for the rescue teams."

"I say we see if we can save anyone!" you blurt out. "It may take the rescuers a while to get here."

If you wait for the rescue teams, turn to page 46.

If you risk your life to see if you can help, turn to page 17.

8

"Let's get out of here!" you whisper to Petyor. Grabbing Gleeb, you rush through the mine tunnel, looking for an exit. The beams of the mine are sagging dangerously, and you have to leap over piles of rubble where there have been partial cave-ins.

Suddenly the beam of your flashlight sweeps across a wooden crate marked with a skull and crossbones and filled with red sticks. Dynamite! Next to the box is a small jar filled with detonators and a coil of fuse. "Hey! This will stop them," you whisper.

"If we don't blow ourselves up in the process," Petyor adds.

"Of course not. I've seen my friend Sourdough use this stuff a thousand times," you say, lying a little.

Actually, you've just read about handling dynamite in a mining book, and Petyor's warning makes you have second thoughts. "Trust me, Petyor," you say, trying to sound confident.

*If you go ahead with your plan,
turn to page 43.*

*If you decide you're better off not using the
dynamite, turn to page 51.*

10

You, Gleeb, and Petyor desperately try to push aside the rocks in front of you. "The entrance can only be a few yards in front of us," you gasp.

Then Gleeb begins humming. In the weak light of your flashlight, you see Gleeb extend a probe and poke at some old boards that have been uncovered by the cave-in. They're so rotten, Gleeb is able to break through them in just seconds. Gleeb rolls into the darkness beyond, and you and Petyor follow.

The smell in this part of the mine is very stale and musty. Dust floats in the beam of your flashlight.

Gleeb is chanting mechanically, as if reading out of a textbook. "Very great concentration of metallic ore here. Atomic weight 197.2, atomic number 79, atomic symbol, Au. My data banks say that it's not good for much except making Olympic medals and heavy yellow jewelry."

That rings a bell. "Gleeb—you mean *gold!?*" you shout.

"*Gold* is the correct answer," Gleeb says. "You win today's jackpot!"

Turn to page 48.

"Just a few more chunks of gold," you say, as you swing the pick a few more times.

Suddenly small high-pressure jets of water squirt out of the cavities in the wall where the gold was. The volume increases rapidly.

"Come on," Petyor yells, trying to draw you away. But you can't stop now. You want just a handful more.

Then, before your eyes, the wall bulges out ominously. Fractures run through the quartz like shattering glass. A thousand jets of water squash you and your friends against the opposite wall of the mine.

The End

By the time a rescue helicopter arrives, you and Sourdough have managed to haul a surviving but unconscious cosmonaut from the wreckage of the shuttle. Soon other rescue copters arrive, and the area is suddenly swarming with uniformed personnel.

After you explain what you saw to Captain Dragg, the rescue commander, you point out the site of the explosion. All around a smoking crater, trees are flattened like dominoes.

"Very peculiar. I'm afraid we'll have to take the two of you back to headquarters with us," Captain Dragg says. "You were eyewitnesses to the entire event."

The investigation at headquarters is long and frustrating. Captain Dragg doesn't seem to believe your story about the sphere of light. Then you remember the photographs you took. Suddenly he becomes silent.

"Hmmmm," he mumbles, rubbing his bony chin. "Photographs might explain what you saw. But if the light is as bright as you describe, the film will be overexposed. Give us the film. We'll send it to our darkroom and see what they can come up with."

Later that day, Captain Dragg calls you and Sourdough into his office to tell you that the photographs were blank. Not only that, the cosmonaut has regained consciousness and remembers nothing about what happened—his memory is now completely blank!

Turn to page 47.

You quickly scrawl a note telling the Mounties where you're headed and tape it to the half-hinged door of the shuttle. Then you say over your shoulder, "Come on, Gleeb, let's head out." Together with Petyor, the three of you start climbing up the ridge to the southwest.

"Gleeb does not like to roll over rocks and through mud. Gleeb wants to be carried," it commands.

You'd like to try kicking a field goal with this metal soccer ball, but instead you pick it up and put it in your backpack.

"We'll head over the ridge, follow the stream, and eventually arrive at Pickax, a town on the banks of the Yukon River. If we can get a boat from there, we can go to Dawson and catch a plane to L.A.," you explain to Gleeb as you give Petyor a knowing wink. You are both hoping the rescue teams find you soon, before you get too far from the site of the crash.

Turn to page 40.

You grab your backpack and start running toward the shuttle as fast as you can, leaping over bushes and rocks, tree branches slashing at your face and hands. At the top of the next ridge, you catch your breath and look down on Cariboo Lake. The shuttle, badly mangled but still in one piece, lies at the end of the long finger lake, its nose crumpled by a stand of pines.

As soon as you reach the shuttle, you go directly to the flight deck, where you find the bodies of three cosmonauts. Realizing you are too late, you start to head back to Sourdough's cabin to inform the authorities.

Suddenly you hear a moan coming from an adjacent compartment. You poke your head in and locate a young cosmonaut about your age, rubbing his head!

"Don't move," you shout. "Let me check for broken bones."

"I'm okay, my friend. I'm just dizzy from this blow on my head," he says in heavily accented English. "I am Petyor."

"What happened?" you ask, as you help him hobble out of the shuttle.

"You won't believe it," Petyor answers.

Turn to page 52.

16

You climb out of the mine first. Petyor lobs Gleeb up to you in an overhand shot and then climbs up himself. "Those men will be rooting around in there for days trying to find us," he says as the three of you head out toward the town of Pickax.

By late that evening the stream you have been following has widened. Up ahead you hear the roar of the mighty Yukon River.

"The town should be right around here somewhere," you say. "I saw it when Sourdough and I flew over earlier this summer."

"Maybe if we follow this path . . ." Petyor says and wanders off to the right. Then you hear him shout, "We're here!"

You follow the path and find yourself walking down the main street of a deserted town. Most of the buildings have broken windowpanes, and doors are slapping in the breeze. There are no lights anywhere, and it feels kind of spooky.

"Hellooooooo," Petyor shouts through cupped hands.

"This is a real ghost town if ever I saw one," you comment.

"Where Caspar lives?" Gleeb asks.

Your laughter is cut short by the unmistakable sound of a pistol's hammer being cocked behind you.

"Get 'em up, strangers," a squeaky voice says.

Turn to page 55.

Sourdough disapproves, but you decide to run downhill to the shuttle, leaving him behind. With any luck, the rescue teams with their fire-fighting equipment will arrive soon and join you.

As you get closer, the smell of fuel is overpowering. You break out in a cold sweat, your heart thumping wildly, as you crawl through a break in the shuttle's fuselage. In the rear of the shuttle, where the weird glow is coming from, you hear a strange noise. But your first concern is the crew up on the flight deck.

Gingerly picking your way through the debris, you enter the cockpit. Three bloody cosmonauts sit slumped in their seats. Frightened, you feel their necks for a pulse. There are none.

"I'd better get out of here," you mutter to yourself. Then you hear the noise again, coming from the cargo bay. It sounds like someone gargling.

Turn to page 32.

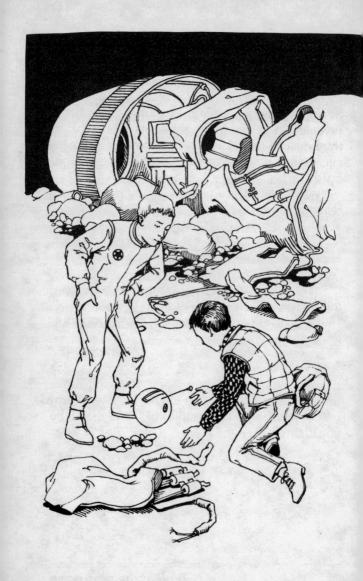

"But where is this 'soccer ball'?" you ask, not believing a word of the cosmonaut's story.

"Here!" Out of the shuttle bay area bounces a metallic ball with a voice as loud as a foghorn. Swiftly it rolls to your feet. A shutter slides back, revealing a series of bright lights that blink in rhythm with its voice, which is emitted out of a circular grid on the bottom. "Gleeb Fogo on planet Earth."

"What planet are you from?" you ask. You reach down to touch the sphere, but it bounces away like a playful puppy.

"Gleeb sent from Ptermania to do term paper about planet Earth." It points south with a probe. "Take me to L.A. Now!"

"This must be some sort of joke," you say, looking at Petyor.

"No," he answers. "This robot caused my shuttle to crash. It is no joke."

The sphere shouts insistently, *"Gleeb to L.A.!"*

"It's not over the next hill, you know!" you say desperately, trying to buy time. "We can't move until the rescue helicopters arrive. Then we'll turn you over to the proper authorities, and they'll fly you there."

Go on to the next page.

"Yes, humans *will* take Gleeb Fogo to L.A. as soon as possible. Important information available there." The sphere starts emitting a low hum, a vibration that slowly gets louder and louder. You cover your ears, but the sound seems to enter your head, reverberating within your mind. Your instinct is to run away, but you are also very curious. Perhaps you should stay and see what you can find out.

If you choose to run away and escape from the sound, turn to page 56.

If you try to appease Gleeb Fogo by calming it down, turn to page 86.

You get Gleeb under control by singing a lullaby. Dr. Wacko wheels in an operating table.

You pass out headphones from the supply closet to everyone so that if Gleeb starts pulsing during the operation you'll all be protected. Then you notice that the doctor has a complicated-looking drill in his hand.

"Hey! What are you doing?" you ask.

"Nothing to worry about," the doctor says. "Just a little brain surgery."

Before you can stop him, Dr. Wacko switches on his drill and presses it against Gleeb Fogo's metallic skin. When the drill penetrates Gleeb's outer shell, a probe arm suddenly springs out. In one sweep, it knocks all the headsets off you and the others. Besides being paralyzed by the throbbing pulse in your brain, you notice a poisonous green gas starting to seep out from the hole in Gleeb's skin. And it smells *awful.*

"Augggggggggh!" you cry, as everything around you is rapidly shrouded in a green mist. Your final thoughts before you collapse are of Sourdough and his warning, "Make one mistake up here and it'll be your last." You've made several, you realize, but you don't have to live with that knowledge for much longer.

The End

22

Down the highway you see a large town looming in the distance. If the three of you can just get there, you'll definitely be able to lose your pursuers in the urban traffic. Who knows, maybe you'll be able to get police protection.

But what's going on? you wonder. As you approach the town, the road is lined with cheering people. They wave balloons and flags. Banners dot the crowd. You can't read them because of how fast you're going.

Suddenly the road ahead looks different. It must be some sort of hill, you gather. Petyor can't slow down to find out—your pursuers are still behind you!

"Oh, nooooo!" you scream as the three of you head up a very long ramp. Too late! You're committed to making the jump.

In the blink of an eye you fly off the ramp. Row upon row of brand-new trucks flash beneath you. You hit the down ramp, then come to a screeching halt. You're safe!

Turn to page 28.

"I compute the word *feelings*," Gleeb replies. "On our planet we have soft bodies and feelings when we're young, like humans. But after we live four hundred years as flesh and blood, a Ptermanian computer copies our brain, memories, and personality, along with vast stores of extra information. Then our computerized self-clones are assigned to explore space and study other civilizations. It is a great honor for Gleeb Fogo to collect information on planet Earth. Even though you are pretty far down on the list of space intelligence."

"So what have you learned?" you ask hesitantly.

"I have studied electromagnetic radiations that your planet emits. This gives me a true picture of the state of your civilization, how your society works, its values and its intelligence. You call these emissions television. From processing television, I now know planet Earth very well," Gleeb responds.

"Uh oh," you think out loud. "But Gleeb—you don't understand. Television is not really . . . well . . . it's not real life. It's not the way that humans really live."

Gleeb ignores you, chattering away. "Take me to Vanna. I want to spin the wheel."

Turn to page 79.

Time passes slowly as you float on the raft. You're beginning to get very worried because the wind is really picking up. You and Petyor keep scanning the horizon, hoping to see a ship or plane so you can light your flares. You hope the *Pole Star* heard Petyor's distress call.

Gleeb, on the other hand, pops in and out of the water having a wonderful time doing seal imitations.

The sky has gotten very black, and whitecaps now whip across the pontoons of your rubber dinghy. The water is freezing cold, and you don't have any survival suits to shield you from hypothermia. Your strength is fading rapidly.

Then, roaring out of the dark, you see a killer wave, its crest foaming white, cascading down on top of you.

The last thought you have as you are engulfed by the wave and sucked under the frigid waters is that you have missed the great chance of writing the story of your short life and your adventures with Gleeb Fogo.

The End

"I just hope I can fly this thing," you mumble as you fire up the engine of the float plane. You've already had fifteen hours of flight instruction in a Piper Cub, but this machine is a lot more complex.

The plane bounces along the water on its pontoons and then finally lifts off. Dodging a cliff at the bend in the river, you bank left and head for the Alaskan coast. In flight, you're able to use the shortwave transmitter to contact your uncle's ship, the *Pole Star,* on its emergency frequency and get a radio bearing on it with your direction finder. Your uncle Ben says a storm has been brewing to the north, but it isn't moving as fast as forecasted. He'll keep a sharp lookout for you. You give him an estimate that you should be there in about three hours.

Things seem to be going pretty well over the waters of the Gulf of Alaska. As you monitor the instruments, you notice the fuel pressure gauge flickering. At first the engine doesn't seem to be affected, but then it gradually begins to lose power. By now you're only an hour from the *Pole Star,* in the middle of the Gulf of Alaska.

You change fuel tanks frantically, and start the boost pump. Sweating buckets, you tell Petyor to send out a distress call. The engine sputters a little, then picks up again. The fuel gauge is still flickering. You've got a real problem!

If you decide to turn back, turn to page 82.

If you try and make it to the Pole Star,
turn to page 96.

You don't want to leave Gleeb alone with these two men, so you opt to come along. After a long flight to the coast of Alaska, the red-bearded man takes you and Petyor along to a door built into the side of a hill. "Welcome," he says.

"L.A. is not here," Gleeb chirps. "Take Gleeb to L.A."

"Gleeb, don't use your signal," you whisper, hearing the pitch of its voice rise. "Not yet, anyway."

"This is the most sophisticated and luxurious space research center in the world," the thin man boasts. "We monitor all space programs from here. This is where our technicians are trained. We have gourmet eateries, a tanning spa, indoor tennis courts, and a movie theater."

"What's your purpose?" you ask. You don't like the sound of all of this.

"Simple. We are outer-space consultants," the man replies, his smile showing several buckteeth. He hands you his business card. The name of the company he works for is Spaced Out, Inc.

That figures, you think.

"Let me show you all around," the red-bearded man says, grinning.

Turn to page 93.

28

Shaken to your very core, you and Petyor and Gleeb look around at the cheering crowds. Everywhere are banners reading HAPPY HARRY'S HOT TRUCKS FOR LOW BUCKS.

A beaming fat man smoking a large cigar bounces over in his checkered suit waving a bundle of money. An enormous button on his lapel reads HAPPY HARRY.

"Hey, that was terrific! You did it! But who *are* you?" Harry asks. "We were expecting Evel Knievel."

As you are lifted onto the shoulders of the applauding crowds and garlands of flowers are thrown over your head, you realize you just helped Happy Harry sell some more trucks. You're going to have a tough time explaining the meaning of all this to Gleeb.

The End

"We'll work for you," you tell Dr. Wacko.

The doctor flashes you a grin and whips out a complicated contract that he has you sign. "Now, tell me all about this alien," he instructs.

"It is not exactly an alien. It is a computerized clone from the planet Ptermania," you explain. "It is kind of nice. It even likes our television and our music."

"Well, we'll have to see what we can learn from this device you call Gleeb Fogo," the doctor says. He turns to the man with the red beard. "Hustle me up a television set, quick!"

Minutes later Dr. Wacko turns the dial on the television set to a music station. Gleeb immediately goes wild.

"MTV!" Gleeb exclaims, and rolls over to plug in. "I want my MTV!"

While the music blares and Gleeb is distracted, the doctor tries to insert wires into Gleeb but with little success. Gleeb is obviously getting angry at being disturbed. Wires begin to short out, and showers of sparks start to fly.

As if you're to blame, Dr. Wacko angrily commands you, "Control the alien right away or you won't get a paycheck! I need to examine this device so I can get the information it has stored inside. My company can sell it. We're talking megabucks. Think of it—the secret of life, the mysteries of the universe, how to travel through time. Maybe even a cure for acne!"

Turn to page 21.

Getting past the fish is really gross. For every three steps up the chute, you slide back two. Soon you are free of the fish scales and seaweed. You feel like throwing up. And now you're in danger of being discovered simply because you smell so bad!

You look up at the bridge. Captain Markus is standing watch. As you creep along the deck, you can see the crew having dinner in the mess.

You wonder where they have Gleeb Fogo. Then you hear Gleeb's squeaky voice coming from the bridge.

You move along very carefully. Just before you get to the companionway to the bridge, you see the crew lockers. Maybe you can find something in them to free Gleeb. And you do: a spear gun, and better yet, a boom box with cassette tapes.

*If you decide to use the spear gun,
turn to page 73.*

*If you think the boom box would work better,
turn to page 110.*

As you enter the cargo bay, you are momentarily blinded by a spherical ball of light. It rolls crazily across the floor, then rebounds off the sides of the fuselage as if it were some kind of silver ball in a video arcade game. The fumes from the rocket fuel are making you dizzy, and an alarm is going off in the back of your brain, screaming at you to get away as quickly as possible!

Each time the sphere whizzes past you, you can feel its heat. It glows brighter with each passing second, going dull red to cool white like molten iron. Then sparks start to shoot off it, hitting the rocket fuel.

Too late to do anything now—the whole shuttle explodes in a blinding flash. Within seconds you and the cosmonauts are reduced to ashes.

The End

"I have the perfect plan," you say. "My uncle's research vessel, the *Pole Star,* is doing a study of gray whales off the coast of Alaska. If we get there, he could help us."

"No problem," Swift Water says. "Tomorrow we will build a raft and you can float downriver to Dawson. From there my friend Peter Nobby, an Australian bush pilot, will fly you in his float plane to the *Pole Star.*"

Turn to page 44.

"We're not going to help you," you snap back at Dr. Wacko. "Gleeb's here on a peaceful mission to gather data. You want to exploit it and make money for your own greedy purposes," you say angrily. "We're taking it to L.A. for a little vacation."

"Take us to the nearest airport," orders Petyor.

Dr. Wacko just chuckles. "I can see we don't understand each other. Maybe a change in vacation plans will bring you to your senses."

Before you can do anything, armed guards hustle you down a corridor and lock you in a dark, slimy cell. Days pass. You're fed nothing but oatmeal and water.

"Gleeb losing power," Gleeb says one day.

"What do you mean?" you ask.

"Must have sunlight to regenerate power source," Gleeb answers in a mechanical croak.

The only lock you've ever picked was on your piggy bank when you were a kid, but it's worth a try. You quickly hatch a plan. You tell Gleeb everything you know about locks. After many slow, deliberate clicks of its probe, Gleeb does it—the door finally swings open. You peer out.

The corridors are empty. You see cameras tracking your escape from the cell, but you don't care. You've got to get Gleeb outside and quick!

Turn to page 80.

Once in your cell, you explain your plan to your friends. Gleeb rolls over to the bars, and you call out, "Oh, guard, could you bring us some water, please?"

When the guard arrives, Gleeb wraps a probe around the man's leg and starts squeezing.

"Hey, let me go" the guard protests.

"Not unless you let *us* go," Gleeb threatens, tightening its grip.

"You'd better do as we say," you add. "If I give the word, Gleeb will turn you into green slime."

The poor man is so scared he lets you go. Although you feel sorry for the guard, you tie him up and gag him. Soon you're back on the streets of Dawson.

Keeping a low profile, the three of you start looking for that float plane Swift Water told you about. When you find it, Peter Nobby, the owner, is nowhere around.

By now the prisoner escape siren at the jail is wailing. "We've got to leave right this minute," you tell Petyor and Gleeb.

Turn to page 26.

38

Once outside the complex, you run for the parking lot. You try several of the cars, but they're locked. Then Petyor spots a motorcycle. "Climb on," he tells you. "I know how to hot-wire one of these."

Varooom! In a minute the engine starts. This is going to be fun. You haven't been on a motorcycle since your spring holiday at the motorcross trails in the Nevada hills. You climb on behind Petyor, with Gleeb holding on to the two of you with its probe.

The roads are bumpy. Gleeb bounces up in the air but manages to hang on tightly to Petyor's flight suit. You can hear cars chasing you, but you don't dare look back.

Soon you reach the highway. Here you have a better chance to get away, because the motorcycle can weave between cars, something your pursuers cannot do.

Turn to page 22.

You have no intention of getting in a helicopter with these men, or letting them take Gleeb Fogo, but you don't tell them that.

You and Petyor give each other a special wink and head over to the helicopter, making sure your headsets are plugged into the Walkman. "Gleeb," you whisper, "they're not taking you to L.A."

Gleeb gets furious and starts beaming a signal, the vibrations stunning the two men long enough for you and Petyor to get a good head start. Tucking Gleeb under your arm, you shout to Petyor, "Stick with me. We'll head for the cliff over there and hide in the trees."

A bullet zings over your head. Seconds later, you, Petyor, and Gleeb reach the protective cover of the underbrush.

You think you've got it made when suddenly the ground beneath your feet crumbles, and all three of you fall into a gaping black hole in the earth. You fall forever, it seems, banging off rocks and dirt, until you finally splat down into a pool of mud.

"You okay, Petyor?" you whisper, the wind still knocked out of you. Petyor groans, but says he's okay. Gleeb beeps unhappily, but is also unhurt.

You take a small flashlight from your backpack and check out the hole you fell through. There's a tunnel supported by old timbers and a small rail track running in both directions. It's an abandoned gold mine, you finally realize. Far overhead you can see daylight. Then two heads appear—the red-bearded man and the thin man! They've got a rope ladder, and they're lowering it down!

Turn to page 8.

"Are we there yet?" Gleeb asks for the hundredth time. You've only been walking for half an hour!

"It's a long way, Gleeb. It'll take us at least four days to get there. Humans only have two legs, you know," you say with a sigh. You put on your headphones and listen to your Walkman in order to drown out Gleeb's irritating chatter.

Petyor signals that he would like to rest. You take off your backpack and place Gleeb on the ground. Gleeb then begins to protest so much you put your headset back on and turn the music up even louder.

"Petyor, you can use my extra headset if you wish," you offer. He signals that he would prefer to eat, then catch a nap.

"Take Gleeb to L.A.!"

You turn around. Petyor is writhing on the ground, covering his ears, and yet you don't hear a thing!

"Gleeb!" you shout, realizing that the pulse of the vibrations can't penetrate the music you're listening to. "I'm going to listen to my music now, so leave me alone. We'll get to L.A. as soon as we can."

"*Music?* Gleeb loves music! Rock and roll, rhythm and blues, country and western. Rap. Let Gleeb hear music." It rolls over to you and tries to stick its probe into your tape player.

Go on to the next page.

"No way," you say firmly. "You get nothing more from us until you stop beaming that signal of yours. Those pulsations hurt us. Look at Petyor, Gleeb. He's in pain, and you did that to him." You hustle over to Petyor. He's holding his ears, but he seems to be all right.

Gleeb rolls along behind you and nuzzles up to Petyor. "Gleeb is human's friend," it says in a pitiful, squeaky voice.

"Friends don't hurt each other," Petyor explains. "People have feelings. Don't you know about feelings?"

Turn to page 23.

Leaving your backpack behind, you stumble down the slope, back to the cabin. Sure enough, Sourdough is asleep at his shortwave radio.

"Wake up! We have to let the Mounties know that the Soviet shuttle has landed near Cariboo Lake," you gasp, shaking Sourdough awake. Quickly you fill him in.

The Royal Canadian Mounted Police respond immediately to Sourdough's radio call. They confirm your message and say they will forward the information to the Soviet Space Administration. Meanwhile, they let you know that the Canadian Air Force, which has been on the alert for hours, will be taking off with reconnaissance flights and rescue helicopters.

"Quick, pack my backpack with the first-aid kit and some blankets," Sourdough shouts, while he prepares a thermos of hot cocoa.

Turn to page 6.

You think you have a pretty good idea how to set off the dynamite. You fit short lengths of fuse into the detonators and then insert these into the sticks of dynamite. Then the three of you press on, trying to outrun the two dangerous men behind you.

Luckily you chose branches in the mine tunnels that lead upward toward the surface. As you turn a bend, you see a bright rectangle of light ahead— the mine entrance!

Two pistol shots ring out, and bullets whizz past you. Your pursuers have made up a lot of ground. You realize with a shock of terror that you'll never make it to the entrance of the mine without getting shot! Desperately, you and Petyor light the fuses and heave the sticks of dynamite back down the tunnel. You don't want to kill the men, just slow them down by caving in the tunnel in front of them.

Suddenly there is a tremendous explosion, and a hail of debris pelts you. Then you hear an ominous rumble. The tunnel caves in, sealing off the mine entrance. You're trapped. And to make matters worse, you can hear the red-bearded man and the thin man fumbling around behind you.

Turn to page 10.

44

The next morning you and Petyor help build a small but sturdy raft. You tie your backpack to the raft, with Gleeb inside it, as Swift Water and Jack push you off, wishing you luck.

Using sweep oars on the bow and stern, you and Petyor keep the raft running down the middle of the river. All goes well until you hit the rapids.

In the grip of a powerful crosscurrent, your tiny raft smashes against a rock wall. "We're gonna be splintered to death!" you cry out, but miraculously you're able to fend off.

As the waters ahead calm down, you look around and realize that Gleeb is no longer inside the backpack and has fallen overboard!

Panicked, you can't decide what to do. Will Gleeb float and wash ashore? you wonder. Or will Gleeb sink, in which case you should continue on to Dawson to see if you can find help dredging the bottom of the river.

If you beach the raft and hope Gleeb will wash ashore, turn to page 50.

If you go on to Dawson for help, turn to page 75.

46

Sourdough is right. If the shuttle blows, the explosion will flatten the forest for miles around. Standing on the hill and looking down at the wreckage while waiting for the rescue teams, you feel completely helpless.

"I sure wish they'd get here," you mutter. There's no sign of life at the wrecked shuttle. And the strange glow is growing brighter. Any moment now and . . .

"Jumping Jehoshaphat . . ." Sourdough whispers as the two of you look on in utter bewilderment.

"That's not a fire, that's a . . ." But you don't finish. You quickly grab your camera and start snapping pictures, one after another.

A blinding ball of light bounces out of the damaged fuselage, emitting a shrieking sound. It rolls into the trees, casting stark, flaring shadows. Then there's a massive explosion.

"What was that?" you shout at Sourdough. Your ears are ringing in the unearthly silence that comes next.

"You've sure as blazes got me," Sourdough answers. "But I've changed my mind. Let's hightail it on down there to see if we can be of any help to the crew, assuming that any of them folk there are still alive."

The two of you bound down the hill to the wreckage, saving your conversation for later.

Turn to page 13.

"Let me see those negatives," you demand, knowing your camera has never let you down before.

"Now, now. You'll have to take my word for it," Captain Dragg replies. "But let's see what we can do about getting you back to your cabin. In the meantime, I suggest you keep this whole experience to yourselves."

"In other words, you want us to keep our mouths shut? If you don't produce those negatives," you say angrily, "we're going to the newspapers with this story."

You seem to have made your point. "Have a seat," Captain Dragg says, trying to appease you. He leans over to his desk and presses an intercom button.

"Darkroom," a voice replies.

"Sergeant, please tell Tom and Ted to bring those negatives we developed this afternoon up to my office."

Tom and Ted are both big hefty fellows. They enter headquarters not with the negatives, but with straitjackets instead. Both you and Sourdough are carted off to remain in "protective custody" for many years to come, locked in separate padded cells. As the years pass, and your hair turns gray, you begin to wonder whether anything actually did happen in the field that day. But the image of the blinding ball of light and its strange glow always remains with you.

The End

"Not just today's jackpot," you say smugly, "but the jackpot of all time. This has to be the lost Glory Hole gold mine Sourdough's been looking for!" In the beam of your flashlight, the walls of the mine glitter with sparkling crystals of quartz and dazzling veins of solid gold. *You're rich!*

You and Gleeb do a little dance but then realize you're wasting time. You grab a rusted pickax and begin to chip away at the quartz. Lumps of gold fall at your feet. You can't fill your pockets and backpack fast enough.

Petyor is tugging at your elbow. "There is no time for this now. We've got to find a way out of here and quick. Those men will hear the sound of your pick and come looking for us."

Petyor may be right, but the gold is falling out of the wall like apples off a tree. There's a fortune right in front of your eyes. Just a few more swings of the pick and you'll be set for life.

If you decide Petyor is right, turn to page 57.

If you wait and gather a little more gold, turn to page 11.

50

"Let's beach the raft," you cry out. "Maybe Gleeb will wash ashore." Once onshore, you tear off your boots and dive into the river to look for Gleeb Fogo. The waters are swift, and soon you have to give up your search.

You and Petyor walk up and down checking the riverbank, but there's no sign of Gleeb.

"Let's rest, build a fire, and have a hot meal before we continue. We might as well head on to Dawson," Petyor suggests, obviously discouraged by the loss of Gleeb.

You're sitting by the river feeling quite depressed and guilty when you spot a tiny metal claw grasping hold of a rock on the bank. Could it be?

"Gleeb!" you whoop as it hoists itself up onto the rock and rolls to your feet. You pick Gleeb up and hug the little ball with joy. You hadn't realized you cared for it so much. "Are you okay?"

"Gleeb needed bath after getting muddy in mine," Gleeb answers. You feel like booting this electronic twerp back into the river, but you restrain yourself. After all, the little ball is new in town.

Turn to page 101.

"I guess we'd better not try the dynamite," you say. "Besides, if it's damp, it won't explode."

"Maybe there's another exit to the mine," Petyor suggests. "Let's explore."

You hate to move around too much in this dangerous old mine. "This could be risky, but I don't see what choice we have," you reply.

"This way," Petyor suggests.

Your flashlight batteries are dying. "Wait. I'll make a torch by wrapping my cotton undershirt around this stick," you say. "Sourdough taught me this old miner's trick—not only will it give us light, but the smoke will indicate drafts, and with luck, another exit."

Progress is slow. Various forks in the passageways are dead ends.

Suddenly Petyor exclaims, "Look, the smoke's trailing off ahead of us. We've found another exit!"

Turn to page 16.

Petyor explains to you that while they were in orbit, his Soviet crewmates detected something unusual on the ship's radar. Realizing it was too small to be a satellite, they reasoned it was debris left by some other spacecraft. Analysis of the radar returns showed the object to be perfectly round, not much larger than a soccer ball. When they checked with Moscow, the Soviet Space Administration ordered them to take it on board.

"At first it only made weird garbled sounds. It was some language, but one we had never heard before," Petyor explains, his voice awed. "Then, like the sound you get when tuning across the international broadcast bands, it began to speak in a number of different languages until it spoke Russian. When we replied, it talked to us!"

"What did it say?" you ask dubiously.

"It asked many questions: What were we? Why were we there? Why didn't we *compute*? It was bizarre! Then it demanded to be released back into its orbit."

"So what happened?"

"It then rolled over to the computer, stuck out a mechanical arm, and plugged into our system. Suddenly we were powerless: it cut off our communication and took control of the shuttle, forcing our ship to abandon its orbit."

Turn to page 19.

Suddenly your conversation is interrupted. *"Mayday, mayday,"* the speaker on the VHF radio screams. Everyone on the bridge gathers around to listen as Uncle Ben answers the call.

The fishing trawler *Pepita* reports that her engine has caught fire and the crew needs rescuing. They give you their latitude and longitude. Your uncle Ben tells you to steer in that direction.

A thick fog is settling in, and you're glad to have radar. Soon the other vessel is in sight, smoke billowing out of her aft hold. The men on board gesture frantically. They lower their lifeboats and row over to the *Pole Star.*

Turn to page 85.

The hair on the back of your neck stands up. "Don't shoot," you say in a strained voice. "We're unarmed."

Slowly you turn around. A little kid with a huge cowboy hat completely covering his head is pointing an enormous cap pistol at you.

"Pow-pow," he says, and dissolves into laughter.

"You scared the wits out of us," Petyor says.

"Cut me some slack, Jack," the kid giggles, holstering his six-shooter. "Just thought I'd see whether you palefaces had the right stuff. Follow me."

Turn to page 64.

You run from Gleeb Fogo, screaming, trying to escape the incredibly painful noise entering your thoughts. But you don't get very far. Convulsions rack your body. Suddenly the hum stops, and through the hazy recesses of your mind you hear the faint voice of Gleeb Fogo.

"Humans, if you do not take me to Vanna and let me spin the Wheel of Fortune, your time on Earth will be over! I ask you for the last time—take Gleeb Fogo to L.A."

But for you it *is* all over. When the rescue team finally arrives, they try to talk to you, but you are unable to speak, much less think.

The End

"Okay, Petyor," you say, "but how do we get out of here?"

He points up. Ahead of you are rays of sunlight illuminating the walls of the tunnel from above.

"Follow me!" you exclaim as you rush toward them, forgetting to look where you step.

"Ayyyyy," you yell as your foot abruptly steps out over nothingness. You reach out and manage to grab hold of the shoring timbers. You stare down into a black abyss, listening to pebbles drop into the bottom of the shaft far below you.

"Take my hand," Petyor yells desperately, but you can't let go of the beam. The gold in your backpack is weighing you down.

"Quick! Shrug off the backpack," Petyor urges you.

Turn to page 69.

58

"Gleeb, I think you should come on board. It'll be safer," you say as you steer Snorkley back to the *Pole Star.*

"Hold on to your horses, everyone," Sourdough says to your uncle Ben once you're back on board the *Pole Star.* "We've got to vamoose out of here because the *Pepita* sure as blazes will come looking for us, and they've got radar that can spot us in the fog."

"No problem," Gleeb chirps, extending a probe to the wire that leads from the broken radio to the antennae. Slowly Gleeb starts to hum. "Gleeb jamming radar signals."

What the military forces of the world wouldn't give to have Gleeb on their side!

All of a sudden you notice that Gleeb is rolling toward the door. You follow behind, onto the deck.

Gleeb begins making very strange sounds, something like high-speed Morse code. "Are your systems okay?" you ask.

"Yes, but I must go back. Messages from Ptermania demand that I return." Gleeb looks very sad. "No more Vanna, no more 'Dynasty,' no more 'Mister Ed,'" Gleeb moans in a pitiful voice.

Turn to page 94.

Soon the president of the United States calls Dr. Walters. In seconds, the military officers are sneaking out the back door.

For the next twenty-four hours, Gleeb Fogo talks nonstop, imitating all kinds of famous people, cracking really funny jokes, and inventing several new hit game shows. Gleeb turns down a permanent spot on "The Tonight Show" with Johnny Carson. But within a week, Gleeb takes over as host of "American Bandstand."

You and Petyor, of course, become Gleeb's publicity agents, and in no time at all you're rich, working for an electronic metal ball from outer space.

The End

"I'd like to be cloned and go to Ptermania with you," you say to Gleeb. "What do you want me to do?"

"Sit on deck and look into my perceivers," Gleeb tells you.

You do as Gleeb says and look as lights start to flash sequentially, blinking faster and faster. Soon your head is spinning, and you lose consciousness.

When you come to, you find yourself in a vast metallic dome. Around you are strange shapes that jerk spasmodically to the strains of what you guess is some kind of galactic elevator music.

A soft, slimy appendage reaches out from the side of one of the encrusted figures. You move away from it.

"It's me, Gleeb Fogo," the figure says. "Welcome to Ptermania! Get your old probe out and be ready to chow down. Gleeb's famous Gourmet Galactic Goulash is all ready."

You feel strange. You want to rub your eyes to make sure you aren't dreaming, but that isn't possible. You realize that your arms are only probes, and the rest of you is a metallic sphere, only slightly larger than a soccer ball.

The End

You drop to the ground and curl up as if you're dead. You can feel the ground vibrating as the bear runs toward you. Soon its fetid breath fills your nostrils.

The bear circles you, sniffing, then slowly ambles away.

You dare not move. Your muscles are beginning to relax and you lift up your head when you notice the bear galloping back toward you, grunting angrily.

The last thing you see is a claw of two-inch-long nails descending on top of you.

The End

With your hand-held compass, the three of you happily motor away into the fog until you locate the *Pole Star.*

By the time you have told Sourdough and Uncle Ben all about your narrow escape, the United Nations survey ship arrives. The officials on board whisk you away to New York City where Gleeb is offered the position of ambassador representing Ptermania at the UN. "Must visit L.A. on business," Gleeb insists.

What?

Gleeb has it all figured out. Gleeb hires Mr. Lucky Lizzard, a big-name movie agent, and then auditions as an alien for a blockbuster space epic. The only problem is, Gleeb doesn't get the part.

The director apologizes to you privately, so as not to hurt Gleeb's feelings. "Gleeb looks like an overstuffed metal soccer ball, and kids just won't buy that. However," he suggests, "maybe Gleeb could be grafted onto an industrial robot to resemble something like R2D2."

Gleeb is really insulted. You begin to realize that it's really tough dealing with show-business personalities. Eventually Gleeb's persistence in trying to break into show business pays off. Gleeb is hired by the National Soccer League as a mascot—for megabucks, of course.

The End

64

You follow the little kid into Sadie's Saloon and find his parents eating at one of the tables inside the deserted building.

You introduce yourself and Petyor. Your host shakes your hand and says, "My name's Swift Water. My wife is called Still Water, and the boy's name is Jack. We are Athapascan Indians, and we come here every summer to fish and gather herbal medicines. Where are you headed?"

While you wolf down a delicious meal of wild turkeyburgers and stewed rutabaga, you tell Swift Water about Gleeb Fogo and the two men chasing you.

Swift Water gives it some thought. "Sounds like these palefaces chasing you are real dangerous," he says. "You better get out of town quick. Besides, Gleeb Fogo's mission could be ruined if different governments argue over possession. Why don't you get in touch with the secretary general of the United Nations?"

"Good advice," Petyor agrees. "But how can we do that?"

Turn to page 34.

Gleeb loves being on board the *Pole Star,* rolling into the engine room and coming out covered with oil, and then rolling into the galley and coming out covered with flour, chased by an unhappy engineer and cook.

To keep Gleeb occupied, you plug its probe into the ship's computers. "Oh, very interesting," Gleeb says. "Your recordings of California gray whale sounds show them to be very intelligent. Gleeb wants to communicate with whales."

"We'll let you know when we spot the grays again," Sourdough answers, obviously impressed with the little sphere. Not much time passes before you hear Sourdough yell, "Thar she blows!" And there Gleeb goes. "Alien overboard!"

Several hours later, just as you're getting worried because Gleeb has been gone too long, you see Gleeb float to the surface and then pop on board.

"Very depressing," Gleeb says as you dry the little sphere off and spray it with rust remover. "Whale leader tells me that humans actually harpoon whales, then grind up their bodies for dog food. Barbaric! Whales are getting very angry and are planning to fight back."

It's about time, you think.

Turn to page 53.

66

After landing in Fairbanks, you pick up tickets for the flight to L.A., then head for the airport gift shop. There you outfit both yourself and Petyor with sunglasses and Hawaiian shirts. Next you buy three cans of brightly colored spray paint and some masking tape.

In a remote corner of the waiting lounge, you and Petyor give Gleeb a fast paint job. Gleeb makes the trip to L.A. disguised as a beach ball.

"Surf's up," a muffled voice chirps as you dribble Gleeb Fogo down the aisle of the jet and take your seats.

When you land in L.A., you whisper to Petyor, "Meet me by the telephone banks."

To keep from being noticed, you split up when you get off the plane. You walk past several men who seem to be scrutinizing the arriving passengers. But because the L.A. airport is so large, you easily get lost in the crowds.

By the time Petyor meets you, you have made a call to a major TV network and talked to "Scoop" Zonker, the news editor.

Soon a silver stretch limo arrives. Zonker, dressed in an embroidered silk shirt, yuck-green slacks, and multiple gold chains, greets you as if he's known you all his life. The three of you are then whisked off to the TV studios in beautiful downtown Burbank.

Turn to page 83.

The Space Administration officials have finally caught up with you! You would like to grab Gleeb and run, but it's too late now.

You and Petyor rush to stop them from interfering with the broadcast. Together you try to block their path by waving your arms wildly.

"Quiet on the set!" the director demands. You get very dirty looks from the camera crew.

"You're under arrest," the chief official says in a loud voice. "Go onstage and bring us that alien sphere or we'll do it ourselves," he demands.

The director is frantic, pulling out what little hair he has left.

You don't want to hand Gleeb over to these men, but it looks like you might have to.

If you do as the man says, turn to page 90.

If you refuse to interrupt the interview, turn to page 72.

The beam groans and shifts so that you drop another few inches. This is one case where you don't want to take it with you! You let the backpack fall, and Petyor reaches down to pull you up.

All was not lost because there are still some nuggets in your pockets! Which reminds you that there's still gold in that mine.

You and Petyor start up the Lost Glory Hole Mining Company, then rent shovels to passing tourists and let them do the work for a cut of the profits. The two men who were following you are never found, which is all right with you. You and Petyor make a decent living with your gold mine, but it's Gleeb who strikes it rich with a lemonade stand. After all, mining is hot work.

The End

70

In the dark of night, you and Sourdough steer *Snorkley* alongside the *Pepita*. Precariously you exit the minisub's hatch, grab hold of the fishing nets hanging overboard, and climb onto the boat. No one is on deck, so you tiptoe around, peering into portholes. Finally you find Gleeb and Petyor in the captain's cabin.

You're about to rap on the port when a guard walks into the cabin to give Petyor a tray of food. You pull back and hold your breath! Very quietly you tap a message in Morse code on the port. You can see that Gleeb understands your plan. Slowly Gleeb rolls over to the ship's intercom system and plugs in a probe.

"Guard Kowalsky to the bridge on the double," suddenly thunders over the ship's public address system. Gleeb has imitated Markus's voice perfectly!

Turn to page 74.

"I'm not going to help you," you tell the military men. "You're on your own."

Not wanting the whole world to see what they're going to do, the commanding officer demands that the studio director shut off the cameras.

While the captain and the studio director are arguing, you have a brainstorm. You sneak behind the set and whisper to Gleeb through the curtain, "Gleeb—do the enemy attack routine you know, the one from that Saturday morning TV show."

Gleeb gets the picture right away and starts to whoop like a siren. Then, in a metallic voice that sounds as if it were coming over a P.A. system, Gleeb says, "ATTACK, ATTACK, ENEMY ATTACK. DUCK AND COVER. ENEMY MISSILES ABOUT TO HIT US."

All the officers suddenly dive under desks, their hands covering their ears. In minutes the television security police have them handcuffed and removed from the building.

Turn to page 76.

"I'll use this spear gun," you tell Petyor. "Unlash a life raft, drop it over the side, and wait for me."

You head up the companionway. Taking in a deep breath to make your chest look larger, you stand tall and burst onto the bridge, spear gun at the ready.

"Don't anybody move!" you command.

Captain Markus and his first mate look astonished. Slowly they put up their hands. Gleeb greets you. It's clear that Gleeb's enjoying being on board the *Pepita.*

"Gleeb, why didn't you help us when they took us prisoner?" you scold. "You could have stunned them!"

"You warned me not to," Gleeb answers casually. "Besides, captain is my friend now."

"Sure," you say. "Except that your new friend is going to take you apart to find out what makes you tick, and maybe, just maybe, he won't be able to put you back together again."

"That's a lie!" Captain Markus snarls.

"Ah—now I understand who is truly my friend, and that some humans lie," Gleeb says.

"Yeah," snaps Captain Markus. "Just like I told you—your buddy here is a real heavy-duty liar."

"No," says Gleeb. "My friend never lies. And yet you call my friend a liar. Therefore, I compute that *you* are a liar. Therefore, I go with my friend."

You quickly scurry with Gleeb down the companionway to where Petyor has the life raft waiting in the water.

Turn to page 105.

The guard leaves the captain's cabin and heads for the bridge. They'll find out in seconds that it was a trick, so you'd better move fast. You unbolt the cabin door and signal your friends to follow you.

"This way, quick," you whisper, leading them to the fantail. You can just make out the vague outlines of *Snorkley* cruising on the surface about a quarter mile behind the *Pepita*. "I'm afraid we'll have to jump into the water, but we'll soon be safely aboard the sub."

You start to climb overboard.

"Stop!" you hear from the bridge of the *Pepita*. "Stop right there or we'll blow you full of holes."

Two armed thugs start toward you.

If you and Petyor and Gleeb decide to jump overboard, turn to page 91.

If you decide to surrender, turn to page 102.

Assuming Gleeb is at the bottom of the river, you and Petyor head on to Dawson with heavy hearts. Once in town you hope to find a salvage operator to dredge the river for Gleeb. It won't be long then before the space authorities track your escape and meet you with handcuffs, chains, and a thirty-year ration of bread and water.

All of a sudden you see Gleeb floating ahead of you! You yell, and the next thing you know Gleeb submerges and comes up alongside the raft. You pull the little sphere on board.

"Gleeb, it's you. You're all right. But how are you able to move about in the water?" you ask.

"Jet propulsion. Sink by taking in water, squirt it out my probe to move around, then surface by pumping out water," Gleeb explains happily. "Learned trick by watching octopus on Saturday morning TV show."

"Well, don't leave again without telling us where you're going," you scold. "You may be cute, but you still have to behave yourself."

"Look, Dawson's in view," Petyor calls out. "But I think I see an official welcoming party."

Sure enough, the Mounties and officials of the Space Administration are waiting at the shore. You and Petyor and Gleeb are then taken to the local jail, pending an investigation.

Turn to page 106.

Dr. Walters insists that you come onstage and explain what's going on.

"What people have to understand," you explain to Dr. Walters and the television audience, "is that Gleeb is a peaceful alien who has been sent to study planet Earth, and that no country, government, or organization can tell Gleeb what to do."

"What would Gleeb prefer to do?" Dr. Walters asks.

"Gleeb wants to appear on 'Wheel of Fortune.' Then Gleeb would just as soon return to orbit and continue studies for Ptermania," you earnestly explain, looking directly into the eye of the camera.

The studio audience, and then phone-ins from all over the world, start demanding that Gleeb be set free.

Turn to page 95.

"So, you've finally decided to come to," you hear Sourdough say. You realize you're back on the *Pole Star*!

"We hunted for you all night, and when the fog cleared at dawn, we found you drifting in a little boat that looked more like Swiss cheese," the old miner tells you.

"Petyor?" you mumble, remembering your friend being held prisoner on the *Pepita*.

"They set him adrift in a small dinghy. We also found him this morning. You're both doing fine, but that metal doojiggy friend of yours is sick as a pup. Probably needs a shot of oil or something."

Gleeb's sick! Something terrible must be wrong, you think. Then you realize that Gleeb probably had to empty its energy banks to create the heat that kept you alive through the long, cold night. You get dressed fast and go to the galley where the crew is gathered around the little sphere.

"Quick, bring a sunlamp," you tell the first mate. "Ultraviolet rays are the only thing that will recharge it."

Gleeb's lights are dimly lit and starting to fail. The screen that covers them is only half retracted, giving Gleeb a sleepy look.

Turn to page 108.

What have you gotten yourself into? you wonder.

Gleeb will probably try to control you and Petyor again with the pulsations, you realize. "Here, Petyor," you say, handing him your extra headset. "Keep it on for insurance. You can plug in if you have to."

You let Gleeb probe into the outlet of your tape player. Gleeb stops talking and becomes an amplifier. Rock music echoes through the Yukon hills!

Turn to page 88.

You stumble upon the door of a tanning room. That's it! you realize. The three of you rush in, lock the door, and barricade it with benches. You then roll Gleeb into the ultraviolet tanning room and turn on the switch.

"Ah, Gleeb is catching good rays," it says, turning over and over to get an even tan. Soon Gleeb is regenerated, and it's high time to get out of the building.

"Gleeb, you're going to have to use that stunning-signal of yours," you tell it.

"You told me not to hurt humans anymore," Gleeb groans, confused.

"This is different. They will hurt us, Gleeb," Petyor interrupts. "They'll take you apart to see what you're made of and how you work."

"What? Open me up? Look inside?" Gleeb is upset.

Suddenly a loud pulsing signal beams out of Gleeb. Light bulbs pop, and chunks of plaster start to fall off the walls. You and Petyor manage to secure your headphones, cutting off the noise.

Someone is banging on the door. You and Petyor remove the barricade and allow the guards to enter. As they rush in, they stagger under the blast of the vibration and fall to the floor, twitching. You jump over the men. Petyor tosses Gleeb to you with a neat pass shot, and together you race for the exit.

Turn to page 38.

82

"I'm going to turn back so we can figure out what's causing the lack of pressure," you tell Petyor.

But you don't get very far before the engine sputters and dies. "Hold on tight. I'm going to try to land this baby on the ocean," you say, as you clench your teeth and hope for the best.

You put the plane into a shallow glide and, with a bit of luck, manage a good landing on the water.

"Hurry, look in the luggage compartment and see if there's any survival gear," you tell Petyor, while you search for flares. The only one who's not worried is Gleeb, who bounces out of the plane and into the water.

"Look, a life raft!" Petyor announces. He pushes a canvas bag through the cargo hatch into the sea and pulls a nylon cord. "Presto—instant boat!"

"Our luck is holding up" you say, as you tie a long rope to the plane and jump in the raft. Your luck soon runs out as a stiff breeze comes up. As usual, the weather forecasters are wrong, and the storm to the north seems to have caught up with you. You watch as the plane flips over and then sinks.

"No problem," Petyor says. "We've got plenty of water and twenty cans of survival rations— freeze-dried pig's feet."

Life is beginning to look very grim.

Turn to page 24.

When you arrive at the TV studio, you are treated like royalty. You could get used to this treatment without too much strain, you realize.

"Gleeb going to be *big* TV star," gurgles the little sphere.

You watch as Gleeb rolls onto the TV set and cuddles up on a plush red velvet cushion. Your space-ball friend is to be the star guest on "The Dr. Walters Special"!

Dr. Walters, a world-class interviewer, sits on her own plush cushion smiling at Gleeb. After the opening commercial, she starts her interview.

"Well, Mr. Gleeb Fogo—how long did it take you to reach our planet from Ptermania?"

"If I compute the trip in your numbers," Gleeb responds, "about 2,233 years."

"That's a terribly long time!" Dr. Walters exclaims.

"Yes, the traffic was awful," Gleeb chirps.

Gleeb is really playing it cute, you think. Then, out of the corner of your eye, you spot a group of five hulking men in military uniforms moving in your direction.

Turn to page 68.

"We're sure glad you got here in time. We thought she'd blow any minute," the captain yells up to Uncle Ben. After the crew scrambles up the boarding ladder, they pull machine guns out of their duffel bags. Most of them are pointed at you.

"Give us the alien. We know you have it because we have been monitoring your radio transmissions since you left the Yukon," says a bald man wearing a leather coat. "And we're taking the Russian space cadet here as hostage, too."

"Who are you guys, and who are you working for?" you demand.

"I am Markus, naval commander of Spaced Out, Inc. Our organization travels around the world monitoring space launches and satellite communications. What we learn from one country's space secrets, we sell to another, for a price, of course. You might say we are space consultants. We do very advanced space research, and we're taking the alien you have on board to further our studies."

Turn to page 87.

"Okay, okay, you win," you say to Gleeb Fogo, trying to appease it.

"Win what?" Gleeb asks, abruptly changing to a chirping little voice. "Showcase number 1, or Showcase number 2?"

"Huh?!" you exclaim. "How do you know that expression? Have you been watching TV from space?"

"You bet your sweet bippee," it responds. "Gleeb loves TV. Gleeb loves movies. Gleeb loves Los Angeles."

"Petyor, are you all right?" you ask, noticing him shake his head.

"I am not hurting. Only—how do you say it in English—I am very confused. You see what I mean by bizarre."

"Take Gleeb to L.A.!" The shrieks from the metallic sphere almost knock you over.

"All right," you answer. "We're going."

Turn to page 14.

"But Gleeb doesn't really know anything except for its knowledge of television," you lie. "Gleeb's just a sophisticated video tape recorder."

Gleeb obviously isn't pleased with your description. "Gleeb not dumb. Gleeb knows the secrets of the universe, the answer to life, and even how to cure acne."

"Ah ha!" smirks Markus. "Just as I thought. That little ball will make millions of bucks for Spaced Out, Inc."

You watch helplessly as Markus's crew carry Gleeb and Petyor away. "Don't follow us," Markus adds. "We have powerful, long-range missiles that will blow you out of the water if you do. And just in case . . ." He aims his gun at the ship's radio and fires.

Once they have left, you say to your uncle Ben, "Let me have the minisub. I'm going to chase the ship. They won't get too far yet because of the fog. Sourdough can come along to help me."

Uncle Ben agrees. He has *Snorkley,* the minisub, lowered into the water. You and Sourdough climb in and then close the hatch.

Turn to page 70.

After a while you hear the sound of helicopter blades. Relieved, you race out into the open and wave the copter down.

Two men signal back. When they arrive, they're not very friendly. "We're here to take that thing the Russians picked up in space. Government orders," the thin one of the two says. Somehow, you don't believe him.

Gleeb cuts off the music. "Take Gleeb to L.A.?" it asks.

"Sure, little ball. Anything you want," the other man says. He's big and fat and bald and has a red beard. With that Gleeb rolls over to the helicopter and bounces in, gurgling all the way.

"You two want to come along?" the big man asks you.

You're not sure who these men are or what you should do. Your first thought is to get Gleeb away from them until you know who they really are. On the other hand, maybe you and Petyor should go along with Gleeb and find out what it is they want.

If you decide to go along and protect Gleeb, turn to page 27.

If you think you should get Gleeb away from these men, turn to page 39.

"Yes, sir!" you respond to the official in charge. Nervously you tiptoe onstage to get Gleeb, but Dr. Walters gets very annoyed and waves you away.

"Cut to a commercial," the director yells.

"Keep the cameras running," screams Dr. Walters. "I have people calling from all over the world. This will become an international incident if we don't let Gleeb Fogo talk to them."

Sure enough, when you look over at the switchboard, hundreds of lights are flashing madly.

Dr. Walters looks directly into the camera. "People of the world," she says in her superserious voice, "you see here a phenomenon, something never experienced in the course of human history—an alien. Is it right for the administration of *any* country to sequester this being when it belongs to all of us?"

Turn to page 59.

"Let's jump!" you cry. Seconds later you hit the icy cold water in a racing dive. Bullets zing past your head.

You shout out in the dark for your two friends, but only Petyor answers. Then both of you shout, but there's no answer. Gleeb's gone!

Just then you see the *Pepita* is making a slow turn back toward you. The crew is lowering their lifeboats when *Snorkley* surfaces beside you. You and Petyor swim to the sub and get inside.

"Where's that metal varmint of yours?" Sourdough asks as *Snorkley* submerges.

"I'm not sure whether Gleeb bounced into the water with us or is still on the *Pepita*," you answer worriedly.

"Well, we know Gleeb loves the water and can swim," Petyor comments.

An hour later you hear a sharp little sound on the hull of the sub. You swivel the underwater Minicam viewer in a circle. It's Gleeb!

"Follow me," Gleeb taps in code.

But that might not be such a good idea. Floating around in the water all this time might have left Gleeb's judgment a little off. Besides, the *Pepita* is still looking for you, and you don't want to help them any by surfacing.

On the other hand, Gleeb might have a real plan.

If you decide to follow Gleeb,
turn to page 113.

If you tell Gleeb to board Snorkley,
turn to page 58.

The three of you follow the man along several corridors and down an elevator. The door opens into a large room lined with banks of computers. Several men are seated at desks working at keyboards. Your host introduces you to the scientist in charge, Dr. Wacko.

Gleeb starts beeping. It rolls over and plugs into a computer bank.

"What's it doing?" Dr. Wacko cries out. "It might destroy our data bases." He rushes over and tries to pull Gleeb away, but he's unable to do it.

"Gleeb is probably just sucking up information. It was sent here to study our planet," you tell the doctor.

"Soooooo, this thing really *is* an alien," Dr. Wacko says, his eyes popping. "You two seem to have some control over it. Why don't you become my assistants and join our little organization? You'll be richly rewarded."

It might beat panning for gold. But then again, you still don't know who these people are or what they want with Gleeb.

*If you decide to work for Dr. Wacko,
turn to page 29.*

If you refuse, turn to page 35.

"Wow! A flying saucer is coming to get you?" you ask Gleeb.

"Flying saucers are only myths concocted by human science-fiction writers," Gleeb answers. "Ptermanian intergalactic transport is like an interstate bus, only faster. Anyway, Gleeb's work is finished. My superiors say they have all the information they need about planet Earth. On a scale of one to ten, they give it a two. Maybe Gleeb come back in a couple of centuries to see whether network television has gotten any better."

"Golly, Gleeb, I'll miss you. Can't you stay?" you ask.

"No, but let me computerize your brain. That way even though you physically remain here, I can take a computerized copy of you along with me. Life is lots of fun on Ptermania. Gleeb will even cook you up a meal of Gleeb's Gourmet Galatic Goulash once we get home."

It sounds like fun, but you really can't be sure.

If you agree to being a computerized clone on Ptermania, turn to page 60.

If you would just as soon pass on Gleeb's offer, turn to page 103.

Dr. Walters hands you a telephone. On the other end of the line is the president of a company that bottles a chocolate milk drink. He promises that if you let him call his new drink Fogo Cocoa, he'll contribute a million bucks to help launch Gleeb back into space. Wow!

After Gleeb gets to spin the Wheel of Fortune, the three of you are flown to Cape Canaveral in a private business jet. You are given instructions and training to prepare you for space flight. Within weeks, you and Petyor and Gleeb blast off in a U.S. space shuttle.

Orbiting the Earth, you and Petyor are very sad to release Gleeb Fogo into orbit. But every night for the rest of your life, you can look up and see Gleeb flashing across the sky, and on a special radio frequency you listen to Gleeb crooning a repertoire of your favorite songs. Nothing like having your own personal disc jockey.

The End

You grit your teeth and keep on going forward. "It looks like we're gonna make it," you cry out an hour later as you spot the silhouette of the *Pole Star* on the misty sea ahead of you.

Circling the ship, you finally set the plane down on one side of the vessel. Your uncle Ben dispatches large inflatable dinghies to tow your plane back to the ship and hoist it on board. You and Petyor climb a rope ladder. Once on deck, you introduce him and Gleeb to the crew.

"We have a surprise for you," Uncle Ben tells you. You turn around and see your old friend standing behind you.

"Sourdough! What are you doing here?" you ask as you shake his hand.

"I figured that somehow you'd get to the *Pole Star.* So I just joined up at their last refueling port and waited," he answers. "I knew you'd come here if you were in trouble. Now let's go to the bridge and figure out what to do."

You're happy to be back on the *Pole Star.* After you explain in detail about Gleeb Fogo, your uncle Ben agrees with you that Gleeb should be handed over to the United Nations.

"There's a UN survey vessel somewhere in the area," Uncle Ben tells you. "I'll contact them on the ship's radio and set up a rendezvous."

Turn to page 65.

Soon you and Petyor and Gleeb are shooting down the Yukon River once again. Days later, you arrive in Dawson, an old gold-rush town. You tie up your raft to an old, battered seaplane outside of town, then look around to make sure no Space Administration officials are waiting for you.

In a small office across the street, you meet Peter Nobby, the famous Australian bush pilot. You explain that Swift Water sent you, and that you'd like to charter his plane to fly to the *Pole Star.* Nobby shakes his head.

"No way," he says. "There's a storm brewing in the Gulf of Alaska. Even if I find the *Pole Star,* I couldn't land my seaplane safely in the rough seas."

"L.A., L.A., L.A. first!" Gleeb yells. *"You promised!"* It drops its voice several octaves and does a foghorn imitation, blowing out all the windows in the office.

"Okay, take it easy, Gleeb. We promised you L.A., and we'll take you there. Maybe we can get in touch with the UN authorities when we're there." You turn back to the pilot. "How about flying us to California?"

Go on to the next page.

"Too far, mate. But I could fly you to Fairbanks, Alaska. They've got a flight to L.A. that leaves about noon. You'll just make it if we leave now." Nobby points to Gleeb. "But you've got a problem. There's no way they're going to let you take some kind of robot as baggage. They'll think it's a bomb."

You look at Gleeb, scratching your head. Then you have a brilliant idea. "No problem, Peter. You just fly us to Fairbanks. I'll take care of the rest."

Turn to page 66.

Petyor begins to pack up the supplies and get the raft ready.

"Hang on a second," you say. "Our food supply is running low. I'll pick some blueberries." Turning to Gleeb, you say, "Come on, you ball of data banks. You can help me."

Soon you find a blueberry patch with plump, juicy berries and start filling your backpack.

"Danger . . . danger . . ." Gleeb starts repeating over and over again. You stand up and look around. There is a rustling in the woods nearby.

"What is it, Gleeb?" you ask.

"Animal hiding in trees feels danger . . . smells stink of two-footed demon . . . anger . . . doesn't wish the berry patch to be disturbed . . ." Gleeb goes on incoherently.

Then you see it over the bushes—the round, dark hump of a grizzly coming in your direction.

You've read that lying down and playing dead is one way to avoid the attack of a bear. But that seems a little risky. Perhaps you should just leave the blueberry patch and run away as fast as you can.

If you decide to play dead, turn to page 62.

If you run away from the blueberry patch, turn to page 111.

You freeze. A bullet whizzes by your head. "Make one move and next time I won't miss," one of the thugs threatens.

With your hands in the air, you and Petyor are led below deck and locked in a fish-cleaning area. The place is cold and dank, and it stinks.

"What should we do?" Petyor asks.

"Let's look around," you answer, inspecting all the lockers and drawers. You raise the handle on a panel. Fish start sliding down a chute onto the gutting table. You close it quickly.

"This is it!" You grin mischievously.

"You can't be serious," Petyor exclaims. "Climb out through a fish chute? We can't. The forward hold is probably loaded with fish. How many tons of slimy fish would we have to climb through?"

"But it's the only way to get out!" you insist, taking action.

Turn to page 30.

"Gleeb, I'm honored that you want to take me with you, but have you ever computed a human before?" you ask nervously.

"No," Gleeb answers.

"You just can't plug into my brain and copy me! What if you make a mistake and I end up with mush for brains?"

"You are right. Besides, Gleeb has record of everything we did together stored in memory banks. That will keep Gleeb happy for many years," Gleeb says in a scratchy voice.

"Oh, Gleeb. Don't go," you say, your voice trembling.

"Good-bye, Earth friend," Gleeb says.

A set of intense headlights suddenly begins to shine down through the fog. You realize this is the only chance you'll ever have to see an alien transport, but the glare is so powerful that you have to shield your eyes.

Something like the sound of air brakes hisses, and an intense rush of wind sucks at your clothes. The lights blink out. As you look to the sky, you see a gigantic bus weaving its way up toward the stars, trailing black exhaust fumes. You look around, and Gleeb is gone.

Turn to page 107.

"Get in with Gleeb. I'll cast off, then jump in," Petyor whispers.

Just seconds after you board the lifeboat, you hear shouts coming from on deck.

"Start rowing," Petyor whispers. "I'll stall them, then swim after you."

As you frantically row away from the *Pepita,* you see several men grab Petyor. One man takes out a gun and starts shooting at you. Although you aren't hit, bullets rip through the life raft. Water starts to pour in.

At first only your feet are wet. Then the water slowly rises past your ankles, then up to your hips. You know the boat will not sink because it has some kind of plastic foam core as flotation—but still, the water seeping in is only a couple of degrees above freezing.

Soon the water is waist deep, and you're shivering uncontrollably. All you can do is crouch down into as small a ball as possible to keep your body warmer and ward off hypothermia.

"I compute that your operating systems are malfunctioning," Gleeb says.

You can barely answer, but you manage to say weakly, "Y-Yes, I'm c-cold."

"I can take stored energy from battery banks and make heat," Gleeb chirps, floating toward you. Soon you feel the temperature of Gleeb's metal rising. You curl around Gleeb, keeping as warm as possible. Your mind flutters toward unconsciousness, and then you pass out.

Turn to page 78.

106

"Hey, wait a minute!" you protest to the captain in charge. "What are the charges against us?"

"You are in serious trouble for interfering with the national security of Canada and the United States," he tells you. "Furthermore, you have obviously stolen this"—he points to Gleeb—"this alien spy satellite from the Soviet shuttle. This alien *thing* could be a danger to mankind, and it needs to be destroyed."

"You're out of your mind," you snap back. "Gleeb is almost human. The only thing Gleeb is spying on is junky TV programs."

"That's enough out of you," the captain fumes. "We're going to put you all in front of a judge tomorrow. My guess is that you'll get twenty years at hard labor."

It's time to get out of town, and fast. But how?

Turn to page 37.

At your feet lies a set of headphones you've never seen before. You pick them up and find they're made of the same metal as Gleeb. When you put them on, you can hear very strange but rhythmic music. Actually, it's pretty catchy.

You record some of the music and sell it to film producers along with a manuscript for a movie based on your adventures. Success is great, but you sure miss Gleeb. Many a time you wonder whether Gleeb's Gourmet Galactic Goulash was actually any good, and whether you should have gone to Ptermania.

The End

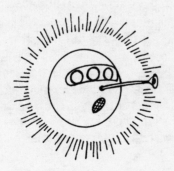

A whole day goes by before the sunlamp restores Gleeb to its old noisy self.

"I was worried about you, Gleeb. I owe you my life," you say to your spherical friend.

"Gleeb was happy to help friend. But draining down my energy banks has caused permanent malfunction. I'm no longer useful to Ptermania," Gleeb moans in a pathetic voice.

You feel terrible. "Gleeb, you're my friend. You can always stay with me." You think for a minute about what Gleeb could do for a living. If Gleeb only watches TV, Gleeb's brains will eventually melt down. Let's see, you think—Gleeb has a powerful computer for a brain, is able to translate any language, has huge memory banks, and can communicate with whales.

"Gleeb! I've figured it out!"

You set Gleeb up as the supplier of fish to all the best restaurants in the world. Gleeb hires whales from all the seven seas to herd only the most delectable and choicest species of fish into conveniently placed nets. Gleeb is a huge financial success until the whales figure out that Gleeb's keeping all the profits and all they get are the leftovers. Soon the whales strike, and Gleeb goes bankrupt. But that's another story.

The End

110

You grab the boom box and cassette tapes and go back out on deck as quietly as possible.

"Petyor, put the lifeboat into the water," you whisper, "while I get the outboard motor."

Soon you hand Petyor the outboard motor and the boom box and climb next to him in the boat. You and Petyor silently row away, keeping your fingers crossed.

When the *Pepita* fades into the fog, you connect the fuel tank to the outboard motor. Luckily, with one pull, the motor roars to life.

As you race back toward the fishing vessel, you switch on a tape. The boom box blares a rock and roll song.

You start circling the *Pepita*. Markus and the crew are on deck looking out. Rifle shots zing by you, but they're all wild because of the poor visibility.

Through the fog you see a bright, spherical shape pulsing through the water toward you. It's Gleeb Fogo, your old pal.

"Gimme five," Gleeb chirps as Petyor reaches out to haul the shining orb on board.

Turn to page 63.

You grab Gleeb and run out of the blueberry patch, hoping that once you're gone, the bear will leave you alone. But this isn't the case, because when you turn around, the beast is still coming after you.

"I hate to do this to you, Gleeb, but I'm sure you don't taste as good as I do," you say, dropping Gleeb on the ground. Then, like a rocket, you're up the nearest tree.

The bear growls and sniffs at the tree. Then it gives Gleeb a swat with its paw that sends the little sphere flying. You hear Gleeb land in the bushes nearby, making a series of incomprehensible grunts. Then a terrific idea strikes you.

"Gleeb, read the bear's mind. Find out what it fears most, then imitate that sound to scare it away," you shout.

Gleeb is silent for a few minutes before it starts to make a whole jumble of pounding and sawing noises. Almost immediately, the grizzly lets out a bloodcurdling howl and takes off for the deep woods.

As you pick up Gleeb and return to the raft, you ask, "Just what kind of sounds were you making?"

"The noises of a real-estate condominium complex being built," Gleeb says a little sadly.

Turn to page 98.

Gleeb must have some kind of plan, you figure.

You follow Gleeb's underwater beeps with *Snorkley*'s sonar for a long time. "Gleeb better know what to do," you comment to Petyor and Sourdough.

Then Gleeb does something weird and starts to emit singing sounds and grunts, unlike anything you have ever heard before. Soon *Snorkley* is surrounded, being buffeted by a pod of California gray whales! You watch these magnificent mammals through the underwater Minicam. Then Gleeb swims over and raps in Morse code on *Snorkley*'s hull.

"Rise to surface and follow us," Gleeb tells you.

For a long period you follow Gleeb and the whales; then in the distance you see the lights of the *Pepita* through the periscope! The whales start moving forward at a much greater speed. *Snorkley* can no longer keep up with them, so you open the hatch and peer out with Petyor.

The whales continue to pick up speed, converging on both sides of the fishing vessel. Then they slice through the water, and seconds later, the *Pepita* is crushed under the impact, folding up like a tin can. She sinks without a trace.

You're astonished!

Back on the *Pole Star*, Gleeb explains. "Gleeb Fogo called in the gray whales—told them that the *Pepita* was a whale-killing ship. They were very upset. Did Gleeb do good?"

"Awesome," you reply, "truly awesome."

The End

ABOUT THE AUTHOR

SEDDON JOHNSON grew up in Argentina and attended Randolph–Macon Woman's College in Virginia. She has taught English as a second language and the Montessori system to 3–12 year olds in Puerto Rico, Boston, and Vermont, where she presently lives. Ms. Johnson is the author of *South Pole Sabotage* in the Choose Your Own Adventure series.

ABOUT THE ILLUSTRATOR

LESLIE MORRILL is a designer and illustrator whose work has won him numerous awards. He has illustrated over thirty books for children, including the Bantam Classic edition of *The Wind in the Willows*. Mr. Morrill has illustrated many books in the Skylark Choose Your Own Adventure series, including *Home in Time for Christmas, You See the Future, Stranded!,* and *You Can Make A Difference.* He has also illustrated *Invaders of the Planet Earth, The First Olympics, Mystery of the Sacred Stones, The Perfect Planet, Hurricane!, Inca Gold,* and *Stock Car Champion* in the Choose Your Own Adventure series. Mr. Morrill also illustrated both Super Adventure books, *Journey to the Year 3000* and *Danger Zones.*

CHOOSE YOUR OWN ADVENTURE ®